D1219772

FOCUS ON THE FAMILY PRESENTS

Inferno in Tokyo

BOOK 20

MARIANNE HERING
ILLUSTRATIONS BY DAVID HOHN

TYNDALE

FOCUS ON THE FAMILY • ADVENTURES IN ODYSSEY®
TYNDALE HOUSE PUBLISHERS, INC. • CAROL STREAM, ILLINOIS

To Katherine Paterson for introducing
me to the life of Toyohiko Kagawa

Inferno in Tokyo

© 2017 Focus on the Family

A Focus on the Family book published by Tyndale House Publishers, Inc., Carol Stream, Illinois 60188.

The Imagination Station, Adventures in Odyssey, and *Focus on the Family* and their accompanying logos and designs, are federally registered trademarks of Focus on the Family, 8605 Explorer Drive, Colorado Springs, CO 80920.

TYNDALE and Tyndale's quill logo are registered trademarks of Tyndale House Publishers, Inc.

All Scripture quotations have been taken from *The Holy Bible, English Standard Version.* Copyright © 2001 by Crossway Bibles, a publishing ministry of Good News Publishers. Used by permission. All rights reserved.

No part of this publication may be reproduced, stored in a retrieval system, or transmitted in any form or by any means—electronic, mechanical, photocopy, recording, or otherwise—without prior written permission of Focus on the Family.

With the exception of known historical figures, all characters are the product of the author's imagination.

Cover design by Michael Heath | Magnus Creative

ISBN: 978-1-58997-879-9

For Library of Congress Cataloging-in-Publication Data for this title, visit http://www.loc.gov/help/contact-general.html.

For manufacturing information regarding this product, please call 1-800-323-9400.

For information about special discounts for bulk purchses, please contact Tyndale House Publishers at csresponse@tyndale.com, or call 1-800-323-9400.

Printed in the United States of America

23 22 21 20 19 18 17
 7   6   5   4   3   2   1

Contents

Prologue

At Whit's End, a lightning storm zapped the Imagination Station's computer. Then the Imagination Station began to do strange things. It took the cousins to the wrong adventures. The machine also gave the wrong gifts.

Mr. Whittaker was gone, and so Eugene was in charge of the workshop. An older version of the Imagination Station was found.

It looked like a car. It had a special feature called *lockdown mode*. The cousins used this machine for their adventures. But it began to break down too.

At the end of book 19, *Light in the Lions' Den*, Eugene was still locked in a jail cell in Little Rock, Arkansas, in the year 1874. The cousins were waiting in the ancient Babylonian desert. Beth held a small yellow gadget with a light that was flashing red. Here's what happened next:

The car Imagination Station appeared.

Patrick reached for the door. "Yikes," he said. "It's even hotter than before."

"Get in," Eugene said through the machine's speakers. "Your next adventure is to find Nikola Tesla. Only he can get us all back home."

"Nike cola who?" Patrick asked.

Beth interrupted. "How are you talking to us, Eugene?" she asked.

"I got Mr. Pinkerton to give me back the computer," Eugene said. "But it has only a little battery power left."

Beth saw Patrick get inside the Imagination Station and then followed him. Beth felt a static shock as she climbed inside the machine. The seat made her skin tingle.

Beth grabbed the knob on the dashboard.

"Ouch," she said. "It's hot."

Patrick took off his coat. He put it over the knob and pulled it back.

The windshield began to spin.

"Wait," Eugene's voice said through the speakers. "I forgot to—"

Suddenly it was silent. Everything went black.

The Tsunami

Patrick felt a gentle rocking motion. He opened his eyes. The Imagination Station was bobbing on a large bay.

Patrick slid his fingers around the door and window seams. He glanced at the floor. It was dry. No leaks.

"The Imagination Station makes a fine boat," Beth said. "Let's just hope it doesn't disappear."

"Yeah, or we'll be swimming," Patrick said.

Beth leaned toward the windshield. "Keep your eye on the coastline," she said, pointing. "Something doesn't look quite right. There's some dust in the sky."

The Imagination Station speakers suddenly blared, "Scientists estimate that the Great Kanto Earthquake of 1923 was 7.9 in magnitude."

"That's huge!" Beth said.

The speakers continued. "The cities of Yokohama and Tokyo . . . Tok . . . Tok . . . Tok . . ." The machine fell silent.

"The Imagination Station's announcer is broken again," Beth said. "But at least we know we're near Japan. And it's the 1920s."

"And there's going to be an earthquake," Patrick said. "It'll be cool."

Patrick watched as the cliff along the coast seemed to rise. It looked like a giant mole was moving under the ground. Wood houses, shops, and wide boardwalks were pushed upward. Then suddenly they dropped.

The hairs on the back of Patrick's neck prickled.

Suddenly a crack in the land appeared. A huge section of earth slowly slid into the water. People and buildings disappeared with it.

Part of the city was gone in fewer than forty seconds. Only a few telephone poles were left. They were sticking out of the water. They looked like straws in a giant mud milk shake.

Patrick held his breath in shock. This earthquake wasn't cool. It was terrible.

He let out his breath when he saw movement. A few heads appeared in the water. Then several people began to swim. Others churned the water, arms and legs flailing.

"We have to help those people," Beth said.

"Maybe the Imagination Station will take us," Patrick said.

He grabbed the knob on the dashboard. It was cool now. He pulled it. Nothing happened.

He tried to roll down the window. The handle wouldn't move.

Patrick opened the glove box. He pushed every button and flipped every switch inside. No lights flickered. No buzzers sounded. No colors flashed across the windshield.

"How can we get to the people?" Patrick asked. "The Imagination Station is just sitting here. It's not moving. The speakers are dead. It's completely broken this time."

The machine began to rise as if to answer him. Patrick looked out the side window. The water was lifting the machine.

"A wave is carrying us," he said.

"The wind has picked up," Beth said.

Suddenly the Imagination Station began

to spin. A loud rushing noise filled the inside of the car. The wave moved faster.

"This is a tsunami!" Beth cried.

Patrick felt dizzy as they whirled toward land. A cliff loomed ahead. The Imagination Station would surely crash into it!

The wave turned at the last second. The water pushed the machine farther into the bay.

Higher and faster the wave rose. Patrick looked out the side window again.

The raging sea was tossing a large passenger ship. A few smaller fishing boats were churning in the surf. They looked like toys caught in a giant blender.

The wave was higher than a three-story building. The front of the machine dipped and then flipped over.

Patrick and Beth dangled upside down. Their seat belts held them in their seats.

"Hang on," Patrick shouted to Beth.

"I am!" Beth said.

Patrick felt so dizzy he closed his eyes.

Beth dangled upside down in her seat. The seat belt dug into her hips. Her hair fell in front of her face. Something white fell off her head.

The Imagination Station stilled. Beth brushed her hair away and looked out the window. The machine was at rest on land.

All was still for a moment. Beth caught her breath.

Then another wave came. It lifted the Imagination Station and rolled it farther inland. But this time it landed upright.

Beth sank into her seat. She looked out the window again. Great black clouds filled the sky. It was dark and smoky.

"Get out," Patrick said.

"How?" Beth asked. "The Imagination Station is stuck in lockdown mode."

A man's face suddenly pressed against the windshield. He was soaking wet. His straight black hair was plastered to his head. His round eyeglasses made him look strangely owl-like.

The man blinked.

Then the door on Beth's side of the car opened.

The wind rushed in with a howl. The sound hurt her ears.

"Hurry," the man shouted. "More water is coming." He motioned with his arm toward the bay.

Beth unclipped the seat belt. She noticed she was wearing a white summer dress. She spotted the piece of white fabric that fell from her head. She grabbed it and then scrambled out of the Imagination Station.

Patrick followed, climbing over her seat. He was in a boy's suit with a white shirt.

"Run!" the man cried. His agile body moved quickly toward a row of buildings.

Beth didn't hesitate. She grabbed Patrick's arm. The cousins ran. The wall of churning white foam raced toward them.

Fire!

A hot, thick, fishy mist was in the air. It coated Patrick's skin as he ran.

He was afraid. But he slowed after a minute of running. He had to watch the tsunami. He dropped Beth's hand and turned toward Tokyo Bay.

The foamy wave reached its crest. The water wall collapsed on a row of wood buildings. The force of the wave knocked down the structures like toothpicks.

The buildings collapsed with a loud crash and a strange, low bellow. Then the wave dragged the flattened homes into the hungry sea.

The Imagination Station was pulled underwater too.

Patrick felt a pang of fear. He and Beth might never leave Japan.

Just then the wind picked up. Another wave began to swell.

A large, damp maple leaf blew into Patrick's face. He pulled it off and turned toward Beth and the man.

They stood together not far from him. Each was bending over and gasping for breath.

The man was young. He wore a suit with a white shirt and a narrow black tie.

Rows and rows of small wood houses were behind him. Several of the homes were already on fire. Red-and-orange flames leaped from the windows.

People ran in all directions, shouting and crying.

Most of the adults carried clothes or blankets in their arms. Others pushed wood carts filled with household goods.

People of all ages bustled through the narrow streets. Children followed the adults or rode on top of carts. The children's small faces were full of fear.

Beth turned to the man. "This was an earthquake. And it caused a tsunami," she said. "But why are there fires, too?"

"The earth moved Tokyo just before noon," the man said, pointing to his wristwatch. The time was now twenty minutes past twelve.

"All the people were home for lunch," he continued. "But their cookstoves must have fallen over. Their kerosene heaters also. I imagine the people were frightened and ran away. No one was left to put out the fires."

Patrick watched the wind lift sparks from the burning roofs. The glowing embers landed on other rooftops. Other rows of homes would soon be ablaze.

Behind the city stood a tall mountain with a brown peak. Patrick knew it was a volcano called Mount Fuji. He was thankful it didn't appear to be erupting.

"What do we do?" Patrick asked the man. "Is there any place that's safe?"

The man looked around at the masses of running, frightened people. Smoke was rushing toward the sky. It mixed with the swirling wind from the tsunami. The sky blackened. The afternoon sun was dimmed.

Beth put a hand on the man's forearm. She said, "God helped us through you. You opened the car door."

Patrick added a thank-you in Japanese,
"*Domo arigato*, Mr.—"

But Beth cut him off. "Yes, thank you,
Mr. . . . What is your name?"

"Kagawa," the man said. "Toyohiko
Kagawa."

"I'm Beth," she said. "And this is my cousin,
Patrick." She motioned to Patrick with her
hand.

The man bowed in greeting.

Suddenly a tremor hit.

Patrick felt the ground shake. He moved
his feet wide as if he were surfing. That
helped him keep himself upright. The earth
rose and fell in a wave. Patrick flailed his
arms to stay balanced.

A loud groan came from the earth.

A fissure suddenly opened between his feet.
The gap widened like a giant mouth.

Patrick's feet spread wider and wider.

"Jump!" Beth shouted. "Or you'll fall in!"

Patrick lifted one foot and fell backward to the ground. He landed on his rear end.

Mr. Kagawa held out a hand to Patrick. Patrick grabbed it and stood.

More high-pitched screams filled the air. Two houses fell sideways and collapsed. A cloud of dirt and dust rose from the ground.

Somehow the people rushed even faster after the tremor.

"The river isn't far from here," Mr. Kagawa said. "We must cross the bridge or the fire will trap us."

The Bridge

Beth and Patrick followed Mr. Kagawa through the narrow streets. They zigzagged through the crowds.

Beth had to watch each step to avoid holes and fissures. She looked at her white shoes. How could she keep patent leather shoes clean in this mess?

She sighed and breathed deeply. The salty air smelled of fish, smoke, and sweaty people. It tingled the inside of Beth's nose.

She glanced at Patrick. Just then a gust of wind lifted something off the ground. It came at them like a Frisbee.

Patrick snatched the round object out of the air. It was a straw hat with a brown fabric band. He pulled it down on his head. But it blew away as soon as he let it go.

Mr. Kagawa kept moving slowly. He dodged carts and bustling people. Patrick and Beth followed patiently.

Beth bumped into a Japanese woman with a scarf over her face. "Sorry," Beth mumbled.

The woman had a long pole across her shoulders. Two buckets hung from each end of the pole. A young boy about eight years old stood at her side.

The woman nodded and said, "*Sumimasen.*" A young child was tied to her back with a pink sash.

The toddler was bundled in a pink blanket.

She held a wood doll with an egg-sized head. Its bright-red clothes and shiny black hair were painted on.

A nearby man said something to the woman in Japanese. She quickly grasped the boy's hand and moved away. The family vanished into the crowd within seconds.

Beth, Patrick, and Mr. Kagawa arrived at the riverbank minutes later.

Beth paused and studied the scene.

The river was wide, swift, and foamy.

A simple, low bridge spanned the water. Three brick pillars supported the bridge. One pillar stood at each end. Another pillar held up the middle. The bridge looked almost as long as a football field.

Short, wide stone posts stood at the bridge entrance. People squeezed past the posts and onto the bridge. Most people had bundles and carts. Some pushed bicycles or pulled rickshaws that had large, spoked wheels. Everyone was crammed together.

Then Beth saw the trouble. Japanese refugees were trying to cross the bridge in *both* directions. Hundreds of frightened people pushed onto the bridge from either end. It was one big people jam!

She looked back at the blazing houses. The fire had doubled in size. Smoke poured into the sky.

"Why are so many people heading toward the fire?" Beth asked Patrick.

"Maybe they're parents going home to find their kids," Patrick said.

Beth nodded sadly. She knew her parents would search for her no matter the danger.

A group of men jumping into the water

caught Beth's attention. They linked arms and began to swim across the river.

"I guess they're in a hurry," Beth said.

"Mr. Kagawa is too," Patrick said.

Their friend motioned toward Beth and Patrick. He clearly wanted them to push their way onto the bridge.

Beth went first. She inhaled to make herself as thin as possible. She squeezed between people who carried bundles, babies, or blankets.

Ragged breaths and muffled sobs surrounded her. Some people called out for loved ones. Others wailed. Still more shouted angrily.

But the refugees who frightened Beth the most were silent. Their faces looked dazed and lifeless.

Beth suddenly felt alone even though people surrounded her. She panicked and wriggled through the throng, leaving Patrick behind. Finally she got to the end of the bridge.

Beth climbed up on top of one of the wide stone posts. She looked over the crowd to find her cousin.

Patrick followed Mr. Kagawa. They elbowed their way to the middle of the crowd.

Mr. Kagawa stopped. He began talking to the people in Japanese. He steered them using gestures and gentle pushes.

He's trying to move people to form lanes, Patrick thought.

Patrick helped Mr. Kagawa direct the people. Together they guided those going east to the right. Those heading west were motioned to the left.

The people on the bridge began to move faster.

"We've helped all we can here," Mr. Kagawa said. "Now it's time for us to cross too."

Patrick hadn't seen Beth for at least two minutes. He scanned the crowd for her.

Beth stood on a wide stone post at the end of the bridge. She lifted her arm high and waved to him.

Patrick waved back and then pushed forward again.

Patrick and Mr. Kagawa were halfway across. Suddenly the bridge began to shake.

Another tremor!

The bridge moved up and down as if it were made of rubber. People were thrown against the handrail. A few of their bundles fell over the side and splashed when they hit the water.

Then Patrick heard a loud crash. It was followed by screams from the crowd.

Patrick felt as if he were on a slide. *And he was.*

The end pillar was toppling. The supporting bricks were sinking into the river.

The bridge dropped with a jerk. One side separated from the rest of the bridge. It sloped at a steep angle right toward the water.

Patrick tumbled forward. He rolled head over heels toward the river.

He reached out wildly to stop himself. His hand found a metal cable. He grabbed it and held on. He whispered a prayer and asked God for help.

Wood planks slid past him. They shifted and left gaping holes in the bridge.

Patrick watched Mr. Kagawa stumble. Then he fell and disappeared through a hole.

"No!" Patrick shouted.

Now dozens of people slipped between the loose planks. Others slid past Patrick.

He heard shouts and splashes as people fell into the water. Others dangled from the cable before letting go. Many squealed before landing in the water.

A pink bundle rolled in Patrick's direction. At first he thought it was a blanket. *But the bundle had a face.*

He reached out with his free hand. He grabbed the soft, pink fabric and pulled it close.

Patrick looked into the face of a little girl. Her lips formed a perfect O shape.

In one of her tiny hands was a wood doll. She shook it and said, "*Ning-yō.*"

The Elephant

The aftershock lasted about thirty seconds. Beth rushed to the edge of the bluff. She looked down at the collapsed bridge.

A mass of people was thrashing in the water. Their arms and legs flailed in a giant tangle.

The river swirled and began dragging people away.

Beth couldn't see Patrick or Mr. Kagawa.

She kept looking for them in the churning water. She had to get closer.

Beth tuned out the shouts and cries of the swimmers. She couldn't help them until she got to the water.

Beth quickly but carefully made her way down the steep bluff. She stopped right at the riverbank. The crumbled pillar lay in a heap of broken bricks.

Some bedraggled refugees had already made it to shore. Many others were swimming toward her.

She was close enough now to see Mr. Kagawa. He was half treading water, half trudging toward the riverbank. She breathed a sigh of relief.

"Hey!" she shouted and then waved her arms. "Mr. Kagawa! Over here!"

Mr. Kagawa turned toward her. He was sopping wet. Water dripped from his suit jacket and dark hair. But he still wore his glasses.

"I'm glad you're all right," Beth said. "Where's Patrick?"

Mr. Kagawa pointed to the collapsed bridge. "I fell through a hole," he said. "Patrick managed to hang on."

Beth squinted. Patrick was standing alone near the edge of the bridge. He was the last

person on it. He held a pink blanket in his arms.

"Patrick," she called.

He turned. He was teetering on a loose wood board.

"Jump in," Beth said. "Swim. It's not far."

Patrick shook his head. "I can't," he called back. He lifted the blanket high. Beth could now see the round face of a baby.

He's got a child! Beth's heart raced. A lone baby meant something had happened to the parents.

A nearby tree suddenly burst into flames. The sparks crackled and glowed. Burning leaves blew toward the bridge.

"The bridge will catch fire," Beth said. "The wood is old and dry."

Patrick couldn't jump into the water with the baby. The water was too deep and fast for him to swim. And he couldn't go back. The bridge was now in two sections.

"I'm going to swim with Patrick," Beth said to Mr. Kagawa. "I'm upstream. I can jump in first. Then he can jump when I pass under the bridge. Together we'll save the baby."

"You're brave," Mr. Kagawa said. "But let's wait. Perhaps another answer will—"

"Wait?" Beth said. "*We can't wait.* The bridge will burn."

As she spoke, a few of the wood planks caught fire.

Mr. Kagawa turned his back to her. He waded back into the deeper water. He moved toward an old woman bobbing in the water. She looked as if she might drown. He reached his arms under her shoulders.

Mr. Kagawa was distracted. Beth took that moment to slip off her shoes. Then she took a deep breath and plunged into the water.

Patrick watched as Beth jumped into the river. He wondered, *What is she doing?*

Suddenly he heard a trumpet-like blast. It came from the other side of the river. Then he heard another.

Patrick didn't want to take his eyes off Beth. But he had to see what was making that noise. He turned around reluctantly and . . . gulped.

He couldn't believe it. An elephant had

charged into the river. Its trunk was raised. And a man was riding on its back.

The river swirled around the beast. The water foamed and splashed against its mighty legs. It trudged straight toward Patrick.

Patrick gasped. The elephant came alongside what was left of the bridge. It stopped in front of him. Its gray trunk wrapped around his waist and squeezed. It lifted Patrick up. He touched the skin with one hand. It felt like thick leather with deep ridges. And it was surprisingly hairy.

The elephant rider shouted something in Japanese. Patrick didn't understand the words. But he could tell the man was trying to calm him.

The elephant walked through the river. Patrick rocked with each step. The baby giggled as Patrick held it tighter.

Patrick and the child were only inches

above the rushing water. He felt the spray on his face. If the elephant let go . . .

Then he was gently placed on the shore. The elephant's trunk loosened and released him and the baby. Patrick stood on the shore staring at the great beast. He wondered if this were all a dream.

The elephant and its rider made their way up the steep slope. They left as quickly as they had come.

Patrick felt something hot graze his cheek. It was a glowing piece of ash. He looked at the bridge.

Burning planks dropped from the bridge into the water. They sizzled as fire met water.

Patrick looked all around the water and the riverbank. The last of the refugees were getting out of the water. Only a few were still on the riverbank.

Mr. Kagawa was helping an old woman out

of the water. But Patrick didn't see the person he was looking for.

The riverbank and bluff were nearly empty of people. Only a few remained. They were repacking their household goods. None of them seemed to be looking for a child.

And where was Beth?

Then something white caught his eye. Farther downstream, the bank curved sharply. Trees and bushes grew alongside the river. Their branches jutted into the water.

Something white—*really* white—was near the shore. It was Beth's dress. She was hanging onto a branch with both arms.

Rescued

The bridge's planks and railings had burst into orange-red flames. The wind blew harshly, and more red-hot ashes scurried through the air.

Beth watched as the bridge burned. The smoke darkened the already-black, cloudy sky.

Patrick and Mr. Kagawa came to rescue her. Patrick still held the pink bundle carefully with one arm. He held her shoes in his free hand.

Mr. Kagawa offered her a long branch. She let go of the one she was holding. She reached out and grabbed hold of his branch. He pulled her to shore.

Patrick gave her a quick hug. Then he handed her the shoes she had left behind.

"Where to now?" Beth asked. She put on her shoes and smoothed her hair.

"We must go to the American embassy," Mr. Kagawa said.

"Why there?" Patrick asked.

Mr. Kagawa looked puzzled. "You are American," he said. "Your accents give you away."

Patrick and Beth nodded.

"So your parents will be looking for you," Mr. Kagawa said. "They will search there first."

Beth didn't know what to say. How could she tell Mr. Kagawa about the Imagination

Station? Her parents were thousands of miles away. And they hadn't even been born yet!

Beth chose her words carefully. She didn't want to lie. "I guess most American parents would do that," she said slowly.

"But what about the baby's parents?" Patrick asked. "What if her parents didn't make it across the bridge?"

The idea saddened Beth. "What if they died?" she asked. "The baby might be an orphan."

Mr. Kagawa held up his hands. "One problem at a time," he said. "First, let's move toward more open land."

Patrick handed the baby to Mr. Kagawa. Then the cousins followed him to a tramline. The tracks led away from the river.

The smoke was still thick and muted the sun. Beth watched her feet as she walked. She didn't want to step into a fissure.

A strange trumpet-like sound caused her to look up.

Patrick shouted, "It's the elephant!"

6

The Temple

The backside of an elephant was waddling along the tracks. Its wispy tail swayed with each step. A long, thick chain encircled its neck. A thin man held the end of the chain.

Mr. Kagawa called out something in Japanese. The man pulled on the chain. Then he and the elephant slowed to a stop.

Patrick, Beth, and Mr. Kagawa hurried forward. They quickly caught up to the man and the gray beast.

"Hi," Beth said. "I'm Beth. And this is Patrick."

Patrick bowed. "Thank you for allowing your elephant to save me," he said.

The man smiled.

Mr. Kagawa introduced himself too.

The man nodded. He was wearing loose, dark work clothes. He spoke in broken English. "I'm the zookeeper Torizo Fukui *[foo-koo-ee]*." He motioned with his head to the elephant. "And this is Zou."

"May we pet Zou?" Patrick asked.

The zookeeper nodded and said, "Just don't touch his ears. He doesn't like that."

Patrick and Beth patted the elephant's trunk. Its long nose curved into an upside-down question mark. It wrapped around Patrick's shoulders.

Then the long, hose-like nose sniffed Beth's hair. She giggled.

"What happened to you and Zou?" Patrick asked Mr. Fukui.

The man told his story in Japanese. Then Mr. Kagawa translated it into English for Patrick and Beth.

"The zoo caught on fire," Mr. Kagawa said. "The only animal Mr. Fukui could release was this elephant. It couldn't move because it was so scared. Mr. Fukui led Zou out of the zoo with the chain."

"So all the other animals died?" Beth asked.

The zookeeper nodded. "But maybe some birds flew away," he said.

Beth felt sad for all the people and animals that had died.

After that, the small group walked in silence. Soon they came to the end of the tracks.

Beth could see a large open space nearby.

It surrounded a building with a tile roof. A second tall, red building stood in the distance.

The area was already swarming with hundreds of refugees. Bedding was spread out over most of the grass. Small cookstoves warmed pots filled with rice or soup.

Little boys played underneath large pines. They made toys out of sticks and rocks.

"Let's stop here at the temple," Mr. Kagawa said. "Perhaps this will be a place Zou can stay."

"What kind of temple is it?" Patrick asked.

"This temple is Shinto," Mr. Kagawa said. "It's the ancient religion of the Japanese."

"Who is Shinto?" Beth asked.

Mr. Kagawa chuckled. "Shinto isn't a person like Buddha or Jesus," he said. "Shinto means 'the way of the gods.' It has many, many gods called *kami*. They are more like spirits of nature than people."

"Are you Shinto?" Beth asked.

Mr. Kagawa shook his head. "I'm part of the Friends of Jesus movement," he said. "There are a few of us in Japan. We sow the seeds of God's peace and forgiveness."

Zou raised his trunk. It swung back and forth like a snake being charmed. The end of his nose flared open and shut.

Suddenly the elephant bolted. The quick movement jerked the chain. It slipped through the zookeeper's fingers.

Zou was free.

Chibi-chan

"Watch out!" shouted Mr. Kagawa. He pressed the baby into Patrick's arms and chased Zou.

But Zou was too fast. The large gray animal took great strides toward the temple grounds. He headed for the center of the garden.

The refugees jumped up and screamed. Men and women snatched up their bedding and children. They pushed their carts out of Zou's way.

The elephant stopped at the large pond surrounding the temple. He plunged his trunk into the water and drank.

Beth caught up with Mr. Kagawa and the elephant.

Mr. Fukui came too. He stood next to Zou and motioned for people to stay back.

Now that Zou had water, he was calm again. The people settled down too.

Beth looked more carefully at the temple. It was one of the most elegant buildings she had ever seen.

The temple was painted red and gold. The corners of the roof pointed upward. It was as if someone had lifted the edges of a tile blanket.

The nearby trees were trimmed neatly. Some reminded Beth of lollipops. The trunks were tall and thin. At the top of each was a large clump of branches.

In front of the temple was a wide gate. Its iron doors were locked.

Mr. Kagawa went to the gate. He rattled the iron bars. Then he shouted something in Japanese.

A man came out of the temple. Beth guessed he was the priest.

The man wore a beautiful kimono. The fabric had a forest scene woven into it. His hair was in a ponytail on the top back of his head. It looked like someone had chopped off the end with garden shears.

Mr. Kagawa pressed his face against the bars of the gate. "Why aren't you helping these people?" he asked the priest in English. "They need food and clean water. They need tents."

The priest eyed Beth. He didn't seem pleased that she was there.

"The kami will help them, Mr. Kagawa," the priest said in English. He made no move to open the gate. "The water that flows inside the temple is for purification. Should I let the refugees pollute it?"

"If you want to be pure," Mr. Kagawa said, "take care of the poor. Especially the widows and children."

The priest looked at Beth again and scowled.

"No children inside," the priest said.

"*Or troublemakers.* The temple is closed. Guards are here to keep the people out. The refugees will have to find help somewhere else."

"There is no 'somewhere else,'" Mr. Kagawa said. "I've just come from Honjo. The entire region is burning."

The priest sniffed the air. "The kami of wind and fire are angry," he said. "I must go sacrifice to them."

"Wait," Mr. Kagawa said. He pointed to the tall red building behind the temple. "Isn't that a shrine to the kami of mercy?"

The priest nodded.

"Then show that you value her," Mr. Kagawa said. "Show mercy to these people."

The priest gave a harrumph. Then he said, "I will consider your words." The priest went back inside the temple.

Just then the earth shook.

● ● ●

Patrick leaned against a pine during the aftershock. The tree helped keep him upright. The refugees in the temple garden started to run. Some shrieked in fear.

The noise woke the child in Patrick's arms. She reached up with one tiny hand and touched Patrick's nose. She waved the doll and said, "*Ning-yō.*"

"Yes," Patrick said. "That's a doll. At least I think that's what you said."

He looked at the girl and wondered, *What should we call you?* He remembered a name he'd heard on a Japanese TV program. "*Chibi-chan,*" he whispered. "It means 'short stuff.'"

Patrick felt moisture. A misty spray of water

lightly covered him and the baby. Chibi-chan grinned and showed four teeth.

Patrick looked around for the source of the mist. Zou was squirting it from his trunk. Japanese children were squealing with delight. They danced in the cool spray.

Mr. Fukui was laughing. He seemed almost happy.

Suddenly the mood in the garden lifted. The scared, tired, soot-covered refugees gathered round Zou. One woman offered Mr. Fukui a cup of tea.

The zookeeper bowed and accepted the drink.

A young woman approached Patrick. She was wearing dark, loose clothing. Her long black hair hung in a single braid down her back. She motioned with her arms toward the baby. Patrick guessed she wanted to hold Chibi-chan.

But something held him back. He clutched Chibi-chan close. He asked, "Are you her mother?"

The woman shrugged and said something in Japanese. Again she motioned that she wanted to hold Chibi-chan.

Patrick shook his head. The woman started shouting. She took hold of the blanket and pulled.

Patrick pulled back.

People from the crowd gathered round. They grasped at Patrick and Chibi-chan with their hands.

Patrick felt trapped. "Help!" he called. "Mr. Kagawa! Help! Beth!"

The American
Embassy

Beth heard Patrick call for help. "Come on," she said to Mr. Kagawa. She rushed away from the gate toward the pond.

Mr. Kagawa followed in the same direction.

Beth saw a small group near Patrick. A woman with a long braid was shouting at him. Others were pushing him.

The rest happened as if Beth were watching in slow motion.

Zou lifted his long, wrinkled trunk.

Pfffttt.

A blast of water pelted the woman with the braid.

The woman shouted, "Yiii."

The stream of water pushed her back and away from Patrick. The rest of the crowd moved away too.

Patrick turned his back to the spray and held the baby close. Then he managed to move behind Mr. Kagawa.

Beth came to stand next to him.

Mr. Fukui scolded Zou. He picked up the chain. He pulled the elephant away from the pond.

The woman with the braid didn't seem put off. She rushed again toward Patrick and the baby.

Mr. Kagawa stood still. He lifted his hands with his palms facing out. He held them up as if to say, "Stop!"

"*Sensei!*" the woman cried. She fell at Mr. Kagawa's feet and lowered her head. She talked in a soft voice so only Mr. Kagawa could hear.

Mr. Kagawa took her hand and gently pulled her up. The woman stood. Then she and Mr. Kagawa spoke in Japanese. They talked for a long time.

Beth whispered to Patrick, "What do you think she wants?"

Patrick said quietly, "She wants Chibi-chan."

"Chibi-chan?" Beth said. She kissed the baby on the forehead.

Patrick grinned sheepishly. "It was the only little-kid Japanese name I knew," he said.

Beth took Chibi-chan from Patrick's

arms. "Chibi-chan is a cute name," she said, giggling. In a serious tone, she added, "I don't think that woman is her mother. I saw Chibi-chan's parents on the bridge. She had a scarf over her face. And she had a boy with her."

"Then where are they?" Patrick asked.

"I wish I knew," Beth said. "They must be worried about her. I don't remember seeing them get out on the riverbank."

Mr. Kagawa and the woman finished their conversation.

The woman left, weeping quietly.

Mr. Kagawa remained silent for a time. Then he turned to the cousins.

"I didn't mean for Zou to spray her," Patrick said. "Is the woman going to be okay?"

Mr. Kagawa shook his head. "Her baby died in a fire," he said. "She needs to find hope."

Beth knew they couldn't help the woman.

God would have to heal her heart after such a loss.

"The Friends of Jesus will soon come to help these refugees," Mr. Kagawa said. "They will bring tents and supplies. They will also preach the gospel of hope in Christ Jesus."

"You told me these people follow the Shinto gods," Beth said. "Will the refugees listen to the truth about Jesus?"

"The people will listen to anyone who brings them food," Mr. Kagawa said. "Whether they believe in Jesus afterward is up to the Holy Spirit. The Christian's job is to love and then to preach. That is the way it has always been."

"That's the way Jesus lived," Patrick said. "He fed more than five thousand people in one day. But they didn't all follow Him."

"Not all," Mr. Kagawa said. "But some did."

A cool breeze passed over them. The wind

gave Beth goose bumps. Then the dry, smoky heat returned. She hugged Chibi-chan.

"Can we go to the embassy now?" Patrick asked. "Chibi-chan needs a place to stay. And some food."

"We're done here," Mr. Kagawa said with a nod. "I'll give you a few minutes to get ready."

Beth found a group of Japanese mothers. They helped her with Chibi-chan's diaper needs.

Next she and Patrick said good-bye to the zookeeper and Zou.

Beth hugged the elephant's trunk. "I wish I had some peanuts to give to you," she whispered to him.

Mr. Kagawa carried the baby through the city. Patrick and Beth followed him along the crowded back streets.

The refugees now carried even more goods. They looked like turtles with their large bundles on their backs. The carts were piled wide and high.

One man rode a bicycle with a child on his shoulders. Another child rode on the shoulders of the first child. The back of the bicycle had bundles tied to it. The man rang the bicycle bell. *Ching, ching.*

Many of the refugees wore bandages on their arms and legs. Some hobbled on homemade crutches. All seemed tired and worn.

The crowds got thinner and thinner with each block Patrick and the others passed.

Patrick guessed Mr. Kagawa was leading them deeper into Toyko. The area looked wealthier. The buildings were larger. Fences and gardens separated them.

A few large, black automobiles moved slowly

along the roads. They reminded Patrick of the car Imagination Station. Headlights cast dim beacons of light in the smoke-filled air. Horns bleated and echoed off building walls.

But the fire didn't care about the buildings. It didn't matter if they were old or new, large or small. The windblown sparks rapidly moved from place to place. The blaze burned most everything in its path.

Mr. Kagawa kept his suit jacket around Chibi-chan. It protected her face from the ash and wind.

Patrick kept his head down. But he looked up often. He was afraid he'd run into something.

Everywhere people were running and shouting. The bells on the fire trucks sounded. But Patrick knew they couldn't stop the disaster. There weren't enough of them.

Mr. Kagawa stopped on a stretch of

sidewalk. Patrick looked up to see a grand two-story, white building. It was surrounded by a large lawn and shade trees.

"It's the embassy," Beth said. "Look at the flag."

The American flag was on a vertical pole above the building's entryway. The wind twisted the fabric. Most of it had burned away. Only a few white stars on blue fabric remained.

Patrick's heart sank. No one at this embassy would be able to help them.

A large portion of the embassy roof had collapsed in the earthquake. The roof was tile, but that hadn't stopped the fire. Patrick could see inside the embassy's bay windows. The interior of the building was ablaze upstairs.

A woman came round the corner of the building. She rushed toward them. She wore a dark dress and high heels. A long necklace of pearls dangled around her neck. Her hair was short and styled. "I've been waiting in the garden," the woman said. "My husband and I were supposed to go to lunch." She looked and sounded American.

The woman nervously pulled on the pearl necklace. "I can't find my husband," she said. "Or his aides."

Mr. Kagawa asked, "Your husband is Cyrus Woods, the ambassador?"

The woman nodded. "They might have gone to the Imperial Hotel," she said. "That's where the lunch was supposed to be. I hid in the garden for a long time after the earthquake. I kept hoping my husband would find me."

She paused and gasped for breath. "What if he's dead?"

Then Mrs. Woods burst into tears.

Beth took the woman's hand. "We'll help you find your husband," she said.

Mr. Kagawa said, "We passed the hotel on the way here. It's still standing. Perhaps we may accompany you there."

"Yes," Mrs. Woods said. "Thank you. I don't speak Japanese. I've been here only one month."

Just then two men came out of the burning building. They wore suits and carried large brown cardboard boxes. They set the boxes down on the sidewalk. Then one man ran back inside.

The other man approached the ambassador's wife. His dark military uniform was covered in soot and specks of plaster.

"Thank goodness you're all right, Major Burnett," Mrs. Woods said. "Where is my husband?"

"Almost everyone has gone to the Imperial, ma'am," he said to Mrs. Woods. "I stayed here to save our files. I was just going there with some of our papers."

Major Burnett lifted the box in his arms. "Ambassador Woods is at the hotel with them, ma'am. His office wall collapsed on him—"

The wind suddenly shifted. Sparks began to fly in the group's direction. They all started to run.

Mrs. Woods began wailing in high-pitched shrieks.

Chibi-chan started crying too.

A fire truck rolled past, bells clanging.

Patrick covered his ears.

9

The Imperial Hotel

Beth and Mrs. Woods held hands as they ran. They hurried toward the Imperial Hotel. The woman's shrieks had turned to gentle sobs and sniffles.

Major Burnett walked on the other side of Mrs. Woods. They were linked arm in arm. He carried the heavy box in the other arm.

Beth saw that the hotel wasn't on fire. At least not yet.

The central garden had a large rectangular

pool. At each corner, a large stone statue lay in pieces on the ground. Lily pads floated on the water.

Several men in hotel uniforms ran over to the pool. They knelt down and scooped out water with kitchen pots. Then they rushed around the garden putting out fires.

If a spark landed, a man would rush over to it. He would stomp on it first. If the spark didn't go out, he would pour water on it.

Mr. Kagawa said, "The building's roof didn't fall in. I don't see cracks in the bricks or stonework. This is good."

"The hotel's roof is metal, right?" Patrick asked.

A voice behind Patrick answered, "It's copper. And the greenish stone blocks were carved from lava beds."

Mr. Kagawa and the man bowed to each other.

Mr. Kagawa said, "You are Mr. Inumaru, the manager. I've read about you and this grand hotel in the newspapers."

Mr. Inumaru bowed again and smiled. "And you are Toyohiko Kagawa," he said. "I've read about *you* in the newspapers."

Beth wondered about Mr. Kagawa. He seemed like a nice, ordinary Christian man. How did this Mr. Inumaru know about him?

The Shinto priest had recognized Mr. Kagawa too. The priest had called him a troublemaker. Was Mr. Kagawa a politician? A millionaire? An actor?

Mr. Inumaru asked, "And who are your friends?"

The hotel manager was wearing an unusual suit. It was half gray kimono and half black tuxedo. His hair was oiled in place.

He looked calm and in charge in spite of the disaster. His manners were perfect. And his English was excellent. It was the best any Japanese person had spoken so far.

Mr. Kagawa introduced everyone. Then he turned to Mrs. Woods, Major Burnett, and Beth.

Mr. Kagawa said, "This is Mr. Inumaru, the hotel manager. He will instruct you." He put the wriggly Chibi-chan in Beth's arms.

The baby grabbed a handful of Beth's hair and tugged. Beth bit her lip to keep from complaining.

"Where is my husband?" Mrs. Woods asked Mr. Inumaru. "Is he alive?"

The hotel manager nodded. "He's in the west wing of the upper floor," he said.

Then Mr. Inumaru added, "The American embassy staff has taken over rooms 220 through 226. The French ambassador and his aides are in the nearby suites. The Dutch legion is near there too."

Mrs. Woods squeezed Beth's hand and then dropped it.

She hurried toward the main entrance. Her pearls swung with each step. Her high heels clicked on the tile walkway.

Major Burnett said good-bye to the group and followed Mrs. Woods. He walked quickly with the box of papers in his arms.

Beth paused and bounced Chibi-chan on her hip. "What can Patrick do?" she asked Mr. Kagawa.

"Patrick and I will help the hotel staff," he said.

Beth frowned. "I can help too," she said.

Mr. Inumaru said, "There will be plenty to do in the days ahead. Take the child and stay with Mrs. Woods for now. There are more Americans in the west wing."

Patrick said, "I'll take a turn watching Chibi-chan soon, Beth."

Beth gave him a weak smile and waved good-bye.

"This way," Mr. Inumaru said to Patrick and Mr. Kagawa. "I need help preparing for Crown Prince Hirohito. He is coming to inspect the hotel."

The crown prince? Patrick might get to meet the future emperor of Japan. Beth tried not to feel left out.

Chibi-chan raised her wood doll and said, "*Ning-yō.*" She held the doll in the air and

waved it. It was as if the toddler wanted Beth to have it.

Beth reached out a hand for the doll. But Chibi-chan giggled and then dropped it.

The toy landed with a thud on the stone sidewalk. The doll cracked in half at the middle.

Beth bent and picked up the

pieces. She noticed that it was a nesting doll. But the smaller doll that was supposed to be inside was missing. Beth snapped the doll back together and gave it to Chibi-chan.

"Let's go find Mrs. Woods," she said to Chibi-chan. "And try not to think about seeing Crown Prince Hirohito."

Patrick and Mr. Kagawa followed Mr. Inumaru through the servants' corridors. They paused when they arrived at the kitchen.

Mr. Kagawa said, "I have some business to tend to. Please excuse me." He bowed. Mr. Inumaru bowed. Then Mr. Kagawa left.

The kitchen was large. The appliances were new and shiny. But the room was crowded with tables, knives, and bowls. A row of empty hooks hung from the ceiling. Patrick guessed they used to hold the pots and pans.

It was already a hot day, and the smoke made the air thicker and hotter. Instantly Patrick began to sweat.

Mr. Inumaru handed Patrick a white apron. "Do you know how to roll rice balls?" the hotel manager asked.

Patrick put on the apron and adjusted it. "Is it like sushi?" he asked.

"I'll show you," Mr. Inumaru said. "It's easier than sushi."

A row of white bowls sat on a long metal table. The largest held an enormous mound of cooked rice. One bowl contained pieces of fried fish. Other bowls contained red powder, yellow powder, strips of seaweed, and sesame seeds.

Mr. Inumaru showed Patrick how to prepare the rice. The manager's hand flew from bowl to bowl. He looked as if he was in fast-forward mode.

Soon Mr. Inumaru was finished. He held out a neat, tidy triangle of food. It had a strip of seaweed on top.

"Got it," Patrick said. He hoped he could remember what to do. And how much of each ingredient went into a ball. "I can make some of those."

"Good," Mr. Inumaru said. "We need at least ten thousand."

"Ten thousand!" Patrick said.

Mr. Inumaru put a hand on Patrick's shoulder. "There are hundreds of thousands of people in Tokyo. Most of their homes were destroyed. The earthquake ruined the train tracks. No one can leave yet. The refugees will need food. And they will come here for it."

"Why?" Patrick asked.

"Because the Imperial Palace is just a few blocks away," Mr. Kagawa said. "People will come to the palace gardens. And they'll seek help from their leader, Crown Prince Hirohito."

Patrick nodded. He picked up the rice ball. "We need only nine thousand nine hundred and ninety-nine more," he said. He put the rice ball down. He scooped a handful of rice and began the second ball.

Beth climbed the grand staircase to the hotel's second floor. The carpet was bright red. She looked over her shoulder. She longed to explore the main floor.

She could see a restaurant and a theater. She also spotted an area large enough for a grand ball. All the walls were made of the green lava stone. The light fixtures, furniture, and decorations were in geometric shapes.

The second floor wasn't as spacious. And the halls were narrower.

She turned left at the top of the stairs. She found herself looking down a hallway. There were room doors every ten feet. The wood doors seemed very low.

She and Patrick could fit through easily enough. But the adults would have to duck their heads.

Beth walked down the hall a little ways. She came to room 204 and got curious. She knocked on the door. There was no answer.

She opened the door and peeked inside. The room was pleasant and sparsely furnished. Lava blocks jutted out from the walls in geometric shapes. Wall lamps in a bronze-green color hung over the bed.

She closed the door.

She went next door to room 206 and

knocked. Again, there was no answer. So she opened the door.

The bedroom was similar to the other room. But the wall lamps hung in different places.

Beth decided to look at one more room. No one answered her knock at room 208. She put her hand on the metal doorknob. It seemed warm. She paused.

Somewhere in Beth's mind was a warning about warm doorknobs. But the day was unusually hot, and so she dismissed her thought. She pushed the door open.

A giant cloud of gray smoke rushed out. Beth took a quick step backward.

"Fire!" she shouted. "Fire! Fire! Fire!"

Room 208

Beth shut the door to room 208. She held Chibi-chan tightly with one arm. She ran down the hall to room 230. She pounded on the door with her free hand.

Major Burnett opened the door and frowned. "I thought you would be room service," he said. "We have to send a telegram."

Beth stood there catching her breath. "There will be no rooms at all if we don't hurry," she said between gasps.

"What's the trouble?" Major Burnett asked.

"Room 208 is on fire!" Beth cried.

Mrs. Woods appeared in the doorway. "Give me the baby," she said. "Run quickly. Warn the French and the Dutch."

Beth kissed Chibi-chan on the forehead. Then she handed her to Mrs. Woods.

"The French are in room 242. The Dutch in 250," Major Burnett said. "I'll go to room 208. Hurry."

Beth felt as if she were telling everyone the redcoats were coming. She knocked on the door of room 242.

"Fire!" she shouted.

Patrick was making rice ball number twenty-two. He heard a commotion outside the kitchen.

He finished putting the seaweed on the rice

treat. Then he peeked out the door. He could see the main hall and the dining room.

Mr. Inumaru was shouting in Japanese. The hotel staff was running up the main stairs. Each man carried a pot of water.

Mr. Inumaru passed through the main hall. Then he rushed into the dining room.

Patrick took off his apron and left it on a nearby stool. He followed the hotel manager.

The dining room was filled with square tables. White tablecloths covered all of them. Men sat at the tables working on typewriters.

A frantic clickety-clack chorus came from the black machines. Patrick also heard many different languages being spoken. He thought he recognized French and maybe Russian.

But one thing was the same about the men: they were all smoking cigarettes or cigars. Patrick coughed. He wondered why these men were adding to the indoor smoke.

"Everybody upstairs," Mr. Inumaru said in English. "There's a fire. We need your help."

The clickety-clack stopped. The men stood.

One of the Japanese men said proudly, "The Imperial Hotel is brand new. The finest architect in the world built it. It's supposed to be fireproof," he said. "Some of it is made of bricks. And the huge stones are made from lava. Nothing can burn that."

"But it has two hundred and eighty bedrooms with windows," Mr. Inumaru said. "And the hotel doesn't have air-conditioning. The windows are all open. Sparks are flying in the windows and lighting the curtains on fire. The hotel will burn from the inside out!"

"That's a great story!" an American said. He sat back down at his table with the white tablecloth. He picked up a fresh piece of white paper. He rolled it into the typewriter and said, "I can't wait to tell the *New York Times*! How many rooms did you say there are?"

Then it all made sense to Patrick. The room was filled with newspaper reporters. Their offices had probably collapsed in the earthquake.

Mr. Inumaru ignored the American man's question. Then he began speaking in Japanese. His voice sounded urgent.

Still none of the reporters moved from the room. They all sat down and began typing again.

Beth is upstairs with Chibi-chan! Patrick thought. *If these men won't help, I will.*

Patrick hurried past Mr. Inumaru and the reporters. He climbed the red stairs two at a time. He reached the second floor seconds later.

A member of the hotel staff was waiting there. He said something in Japanese.

Patrick panicked. He didn't understand. "What?" he asked.

The Japanese man shook his head. He said more Japanese words in a louder voice.

Patrick still didn't understand.

The man pointed to a hallway to Patrick's left. Then he made a shooing motion.

Patrick ran down the hallway and into a cloud of smoke.

He bumped into someone and fell backward. "Ouch!" he said.

"Patrick?" Beth said. "Sorry, I didn't see you."

"What's going on?" he asked.

"I've been going into the rooms after the adults have checked for fire," she said. "They shut the windows, and I take down the curtains."

Patrick stood and asked, "Which rooms have you done?"

"Only a few on this wing," she said.

Just then Major Burnett and a hotel bellhop hurried toward them. The hotel employee had a large kitchen pot in his arms. It was full of water.

"Make way," Major Burnett said. "We're coming through with water for room 208!"

Patrick and Beth squeezed against the wall. The men rushed past without slowing down. Beth moved as if to follow them.

"Wait," Patrick said. He grabbed her arm.

"Let's stay together," Patrick said. "It might be difficult taking down the curtains alone."

They entered a bedroom and moved quickly to the window. Patrick and Beth yanked on the curtains. They pulled the curtains down along with the rods.

"I'll put the curtains in the tiled bathroom just to be safe. There could be a spark smoldering in the fabric," Patrick said.

He bundled the curtains and opened the bathroom door. He was surprised to see the water pipes used as towel racks. He dropped the fabric in the tiled shower and left.

The cousins then took the curtains down in about forty rooms.

In one room Patrick heard some unusual noise. He leaned out the window.

"Beth," he said, "come see this."

Beth leaned out the window too. "Whoa," she said. "What's going on?"

A man on a white horse was near the pool. Mr. Kagawa stood next to him.

Patrick saw dozens of Japanese men in khaki military uniforms. They were positioned on the hotel grounds.

One guard stood at each corner of the pool. Another pair stood at the hotel entrance.

All of them had rifles at the ready.

The Crown Prince

The young man on the white horse rode into the garden. Patrick could see him through the smoky haze.

The man wore a military coat. A yellow sash crossed his chest. A striped belt circled his waist. The rest of the uniform was covered with medals, bars, and fancy patches.

"I think that's the crown prince!" Patrick said. "And Mr. Kagawa is walking next to him."

"The prince looks glorious!" Beth said. "I didn't miss seeing him after all."

The man got off the horse. Several soldiers went with him into the hotel lobby. Mr. Kagawa followed them inside.

Beth and Patrick quickly closed the window. They hurried into the hallway.

Patrick's legs suddenly felt like rubber. The building was shaking.

"Another tremor," Beth said.

Patrick stepped back underneath the doorway of room 230. He pulled Beth next to him.

The shifting bricks creaked a little and then the movement stopped.

Major Burnett found them standing in the doorway.

"The staff can take over putting out the small fires," he said. "The crown prince is here. I'm going to greet him."

Patrick glanced at Beth. She was frowning.

"Should I get Chibi-chan?" she asked. "Or do you think Mrs. Woods will still watch her for me?"

"Oh, let's not disturb the Woods," said Major Burnett quickly. "I think they need to rest. Telling them about the prince might excite Ambassador Woods. And he had a fright when his office collapsed."

"But his wife wasn't with him," Beth said. "Wouldn't she like to see the prince?"

"You saw how panicked Mrs. Woods was earlier," Major Burnett said. "I'm sure holding a baby is just what she needs. Peace and quiet."

Patrick was confused. He said, "But a baby isn't peace and quiet—"

"Yes, it is!" Major Burnett said. "Small children are just the thing for calming the nerves. Why, I have several myself. We *all* sleep like babies when I'm home."

Beth was silent. She crossed her arms and raised an eyebrow. Patrick could tell she didn't believe Major Burnett.

Patrick also thought the major was talking nonsense. Then he figured out that Major Burnett was teasing them.

"Oh," Patrick said, grinning. "I get it. You want to meet the prince and represent the United States *yourself.*"

Major Burnett winked at Patrick. "You'll be a good politician one day, boy! History is to be made this day! And I intend to make my way to center stage."

Major Burnett brushed soot and dust off his uniform jacket. Then he gave the cousins a salute. "Let's leave the Woods alone for the time being. Come with me," he said.

Major Burnett turned and headed toward the stairs. Patrick and Beth followed him.

They came to the dining room on the

first floor. It had been full of journalists and typewriters before. Now the tables were pushed back against the walls. Mr. Inumaru and Crown Prince Hirohito were on a raised platform. Mr. Inumaru was standing at a podium.

Many people had come to the Imperial Hotel. The room was full to bursting with well-to-do Asians, Americans, and Europeans. Most of those present were men. But there were several women and even a few children.

Some newspapermen had their cameras out. Others stood nearer the prince with notebooks and pens ready.

Patrick wondered if this was a press conference.

Beth gently nudged Patrick in the ribs with her elbow. "There's Mr. Kagawa. Let's go stand next to him."

Mr. Kagawa smiled as the cousins came near.

Suddenly one of the soldiers near the prince moved. He walked to the podium and spoke in Japanese.

The journalists began writing on their pads of paper.

Mr. Kagawa whispered, "The soldier says the Imperial Palace is standing, but it is cracked. It may yet fall. The emperor and the empress are out of the city. They are safe."

The soldier spoke again. Then the crown prince stepped up to the podium. He spoke quickly and with a high-pitched voice. His words echoed off the stone walls.

Mr. Kagawa put the words into English. He said, "The Imperial Hotel will house the foreigners in the city. The Japanese navy will bring supplies tomorrow—tents, cots, and rice. The hotel is to feed its foreign guests first and then the refugees."

Patrick thought, *Mr. Inumaru was right. We will need ten thousand rice balls.*

The prince spoke for just a few seconds. Then Major Burnett talked about American naval ships in the area. The US ships would bring food. They would also help transport refugees to safer regions.

Major Burnett sat down. Then the prince began to speak in Japanese again. This time he talked much longer. The journalists asked questions. And sometimes the Japanese soldier spoke again too.

A small tremor shook the ground. The building groaned and settled. A tense silence filled the room. Then the prince spoke again.

Patrick felt very tired. He leaned against a nearby stone pillar. He closed his eyes to take a nap.

Suddenly a word woke him from his snoozing: "Tesla."

Patrick turned toward Beth. She was staring at him wide eyed.

"We forgot all about finding Nikola Tesla," she said.

"We've been too busy just surviving," Patrick said. "We also had Chibi-chan to worry about."

"The prince said the name *Tesla* twice. Maybe Tesla is here!" Beth said. She scanned the room. "We don't even know what he looks like. He could be anyone."

Patrick pulled on Mr. Kagawa's sleeve. "What's going on?" he asked. "What did they say about Tesla?"

Mr. Kagawa leaned forward as if to whisper. But just then the prince said something. Mr. Kagawa paused.

"Excuse me," Mr. Kagawa said. "The crown prince just asked me to speak to the crowd."

The Tornado Fire

Beth whispered to Patrick. "Why does the prince want Mr. Kagawa to speak?" she asked. "What is he going to say?"

Patrick shrugged. "We'll find out!" he said.

The people in the crowded room moved aside. Mr. Kagawa made his way up to the podium.

Mr. Kagawa approached Mr. Inumaru, the prince, and the soldier. Mr. Inumaru's Japanese tuxedo made him look dignified.

The crown prince looked regal. The soldier looked crisp and neat.

But Mr. Kagawa's clothes were dirty and torn. His face was still covered in soot. He seemed small and bedraggled next to the well-dressed men.

"The honorable Prince Hirohito has asked me to help with the refugees," he said. "I am at the service of my countrymen."

An American journalist called out, "What are your first concerns?"

"I've been asked to help the people and the police talk to one another," Mr. Kagawa said. "The people will be hungry and angry. The police will be overworked and fearful. We want them to work together to keep the city safe."

"So you're saying the refugees will riot," the journalist said. It wasn't a question. "The crowds will attack the police."

Mr. Kagawa said, "I'm saying that everyone wants peace after this disaster. I will do my best to reason with the police officers and the refugees."

Beth wanted to know why Mr. Kagawa had been asked to help. She took a deep breath. Then she spoke up from the very back of the room. "Why are *you* being asked to do this, Mr. Kagawa?"

Another reporter with a French accent piped in. "What is your background?" he asked.

Mr. Kagawa smiled and gave a little bow. "My life's work is to help the poor. I have been very public about it," he said. "I helped organize the farmers and factory workers. That has led to better wages. I have also lived in the slums for many years. I understand the troubles of the homeless."

Mr. Kagawa paused as the journalists

kept writing in their notebooks. A Japanese reporter asked something in Japanese.

Then Major Burnett asked, "Will the YMCA and the American Christian mission agencies send help?"

"I will ask them," Mr. Kagawa said. "Just as you will seek help from the American Red Cross. I believe they will send money and supplies to feed the poor. The mission agencies will set up housing for the refugees. And they will open orphanages for lost children."

People in the crowd murmured their approval.

Beth was also happy that the Americans would help the refugees. She felt proud of her country.

The soldier near the prince motioned for the interview to stop. The soldier moved to the podium. He spoke in broken English. "Soldiers here to protect you. They keep refugees away from hotel."

Mr. Inumaru joined the soldier at the podium. "Guards will be on the hotel grounds at all times," the hotel manager said. "Tomorrow we will put cots in the community areas. Tonight we ask that each bedroom fit at least six people in it."

Beth whispered, "There's only one bed in each room. That means at least four people will have to sleep on the floor."

Patrick told her the rooms could fit fourteen hundred people. The bigger rooms like the dining hall could fit a thousand more on cots. Hadn't Mr. Inumaru said the city had hundreds of thousands of people? Many people would be on the streets.

Beth felt glad to have a place that wasn't burning. She said a prayer of thanks to God.

The press conference came to an abrupt

end. The room emptied with Crown Prince Hirohito leaving first. Then the Europeans and Americans filed out past Patrick and Beth.

Only the journalists stayed. They sat back down at their tables and began typing. *Clickety-clack.*

"Now we can ask about Tesla," Beth said. "Let's find Mr. Kagawa."

Patrick and Beth checked behind the black-leather couches. They looked around potted palms. They looked down the hallways. They checked the theater room.

Their friend wasn't anywhere.

"Maybe he's gone to another part of the hotel," Patrick said.

Beth looked out one of the low windows in the dining area. "It's dark outside. I can't see very much," she said. "Just some bushes and more lava bricks sticking out."

Patrick pointed to some windows at the top of the room. "Let's go out on the second-story walkway," he said. "The sides are all open. We should be able to see more from up there."

Beth and Patrick hurried up the stairs. A group of Europeans was coming inside. Beth recognized two of them as the Dutch ambassador and his wife.

The last man inside quickly pulled the walkway door shut behind them. It closed with a bang.

The ambassador was tall and round. "Don't go out there," he said to the cousins. "The wind almost blew me away. You'd be tossed about like a leaf in a tornado."

The man rubbed his bald head. "I even lost my hat."

His wife smiled at Beth and Patrick. "You be good children," she said. "You're lucky you get to come inside away from the fire."

She patted Beth on the head. "Go back to the first floor by way of the lobby," she said. "That's the safest way to get to the west wing."

"Speaking of safety," the ambassador said, "I noticed you talking to Kagawa during the press conference. Stay away from that scoundrel. He's been imprisoned twice! I wouldn't let a child of mine hang around with a criminal."

Beth gasped. "But Mr. Kagawa is so nice!" she said. "And the crown prince is letting him help with the refugees."

"The prince just wants to keep an eye on Kagawa," the ambassador said. "Everyone knows he'll stir things up with the refugees anyway. He's a union man."

Then the ambassador, his wife, and the other foreigners left the corridor.

"What's a union man?" Patrick asked.

Beth shrugged. "It can't be all bad if Mr. Kagawa is one of them," she said.

Patrick put his hand on the door's horizontal metal bar. "I'll just take a quick peek. Maybe Mr. Kagawa is leaving the hotel," he said. "I'll come inside if it really is too windy."

Patrick pressed his full weight against the door. It wouldn't budge.

"The wind is holding the door shut," Patrick said.

Beth leaned on the door too. She pushed her shoulder into it. The door opened just a bit. Suddenly it flew open.

Patrick staggered onto the walkway. Beth followed.

The wind beat at them mightily. Beth's legs felt wobbly, but they held her steady. A dry heat scorched her skin and throat.

But the fire was worse than the wind. It

was five times the size it had been in the afternoon. A great cone-shaped mass of fire swirled over the city from the east. It reached from the ground to the sky.

The fire wind picked up trees and rooftops. It lifted telephone poles and bicycles.

"What is that?" Beth asked in a hoarse voice.

"A cyclone of fire!" Patrick shouted. "And it's headed this way!"

The cousins hurried inside and shut the door. Beth hoped the hotel really was fireproof.

Kaboom! The building shook. A series of explosions sounded.

Patrick dove under a chair and put his arms over his head.

Beth clapped her hands over her ears to stop the ache from the noise. She moved away from the windows.

The fire passed the building. A dark-orange

color glowed through the windows. Beth felt as if the air were getting thinner. Her breaths were short and desperate.

Then the glow was suddenly gone.

Mrs. Woods

That night Patrick and Beth slept on the floor of room 242. Chibi-chan lay curled in a ball between the cousins. They used the silk window curtains as blankets. Patrick's back was pressed against the wall. He woke when Chibi-chan bonked him on the head with her doll.

"*Ning-yō*," the toddler said.

"Ouch," Patrick said. "Stop that."

Chibi-chan giggled. She threw the doll

against the wall. It split perfectly in half around the middle.

"She broke the doll," Patrick said. "Though it's strange that it broke in a straight line. And it's hollow."

Beth sat up. Her hair was a tangled mess. "It's a nesting doll," she said. "It's supposed to open up and have a smaller doll inside."

Beth fitted the doll back together. She handed it to Chibi-chan. "Keep your doll in one piece," she said to the toddler. "You've already lost the smaller doll that fits inside."

Chibi-chan snatched the doll and shook it.

Beth smiled and looked at Patrick. "It's a miracle we didn't get burned up," she said. "The hotel is still standing even after the fire tornado."

Patrick yawned. "I didn't sleep much," he said. "The whistling wind was eerie. The clanging of the fire-truck bells went on all night. And the shouts from the hotel staff reminded me of the fire."

Beth nodded. "The men were up all night with their buckets," she said. "I kind of wish we could have gone out there too."

The bedroom door opened. Mrs. Woods poked her head through the doorway. "They need help in the kitchen," she said. "Mr. Inumaru asked for you two."

Ambassador and Mrs. Woods had been kind to Chibi-chan and the cousins. The children had been allowed to share the ambassador's room. But Mr. Woods had never even been there. The American embassy staff had worked all night in room 244.

Chibi-chan crawled toward Mrs. Woods. The woman stepped into the room. She picked up the baby. Chibi-chan pulled on Mrs. Woods's pearl necklace.

"I'll see that this little one gets clean," Mrs. Woods said. "But then you'll need to take her to Mr. Kagawa. I hope he can find her parents."

If they're still alive, Patrick thought. He felt sad.

"Mr. Kagawa?" Beth said. "Where is he?"

"He's already outside managing the refugees," she said. "And thank goodness. The homeless would break into the hotel if he weren't there. Mr. Kagawa certainly has a way with the Japanese people. They love him so."

Patrick remembered what the Dutch ambassador had said about Mr. Kagawa. Not everyone liked him. Patrick asked, "What's a union man?"

Mrs. Woods laughed. "A union man gets paid to organize labor groups. Like farmers and factory workers."

"Is that what Mr. Kagawa does?" Patrick asked. He stood and stretched.

Beth was folding the curtains neatly.

"Not really," Mrs. Woods said. "Mr. Kagawa is more like a pastor. He studied in America. Now he helps the laborers organize themselves. He teaches them to work together in love. And to look out for one another. One way to do that is for workers to demand higher wages. Sometimes that makes the government angry."

"Does Mr. Kagawa get paid?" Beth asked.

Mrs. Woods shook her head. "Mercy, no," she said. "He *gives money away*. Lots of it. He became a famous author while he was in prison."

Chibi-chan started to whine. "Oh dear," Mrs. Woods said. "She needs breakfast. But first she needs cleaning up." Mrs. Woods took the baby into the bathroom.

Patrick's stomach growled. He was hungry too. "I wonder if they'll let us have something to eat," he said.

Beth patted her stomach. "I hope so," she said.

Mrs. Woods returned with Chibi-chan. She smiled and said, "Mr. Inumaru made sure there is food for guests. Go to the small dining room on the first floor. There's breakfast for the foreign-embassy staffs, guests, and Japanese officials."

Fifteen minutes later, Patrick and Beth found the dining room. Some of the journalists and Japanese officials were already seated at tables.

Patrick held Chibi-chan in one arm. He balanced her on his hip. The wood doll was in her hand. Chibi-chan shook it.

"*Ning-yō*," the toddler said.

Each child in the room was given a bowl. It held a cold rice mixture.

Beth carried her bowl and Chibi-chan's. They sat down at a dining table. The backs of the chairs were orange and diamond shaped.

"I think that's tofu," Beth said, looking at her bowl. She poked at a white, square chunk with a pair of chopsticks.

"What's tofu?" Patrick asked.

"It's like soybean Jell-O," Beth said. "I've had it at restaurants."

Patrick wrinkled his nose. He would never eat this at home. But he was so hungry, he gobbled down the entire bowl.

Beth fed Chibi-chan with chopsticks. Not too much fell off. The toddler ate several chunks of bean curd.

Patrick felt a hand on his shoulder. He turned around.

Mr. Inumaru was standing beside him.

"From the US Navy," the manager said. "A supply ship from the Philippines arrived this morning."

He placed a tin of canned meat  on their table. "Sorry you can have only one. I wish we had one for each visitor."

Patrick gave Beth a smile. They knew two more meat tins were in Babylon. Patrick wondered about the yellow electric gadget from their last adventure. Where was it?

"Thanks, Mr. Inumaru," Beth and Patrick said at the same time.

"No free breakfast," the manager said. "I need help with the Tesla generator."

Patrick's heart leaped. *Tesla!*

Beth's chopsticks froze halfway to Chibi-chan's mouth. She asked, "Did you say Tesla?"

Mr. Inumaru nodded. "All the kitchen stoves are electric," he said. "The hotel owner bought the best backup generator money could buy. A Westinghouse alternating-current generator. It was designed by Nikola Tesla. The prince wants to see the generator working."

Patrick frowned. "So Tesla isn't at the hotel," he said.

Mr. Inumaru gave Patrick an odd look. "Mr. Tesla lives in New York," the manager said. "We both lived at the Waldorf Astoria hotel during the Great War."

Beth dropped her chopsticks and then stood. "You know Mr. Tesla *personally*?"

"Yes," Mr. Inumaru said. "I know many famous Americans. That's how I got this job. The Astoria is one of the ritzy New York hotels. I was the assistant manager there. I learned how to take care of rich foreigners."

"Then Mr. Tesla is rich?" Patrick asked.

"Not exactly," Mr. Inumaru said. "He has rich friends . . ." He held up his hands. "Tesla isn't important now. We need to hook up the generator to cook more rice. The crown prince wants food for the refugees."

Beth and Patrick looked at each other.

"It's your turn to hold Chibi-chan," Beth said to her cousin. She crossed her arms.

"But you got to see the crown prince. You also got to warn the ambassadors about the fire," Patrick said. "I only got to make rice balls. So you didn't miss anything when it was your turn to take care—"

"But at least I took a turn," Beth said. "You haven't had one."

"Children," Mr. Inumaru said. "Please choose . . ."

Patrick sighed. "Okay," he said. "I'll take Chibi-chan to Mr. Kagawa. You can help with the generator." He lifted the child out of the dining chair.

Beth kissed Chibi-chan on the cheek as a good-bye. She whispered thanks to Patrick. Then she turned toward the hotel manager.

Patrick waved to Beth as she and Mr. Inumaru left the dining room.

14

The Missing Doll

Beth followed Mr. Inumaru out of the dining room.

They passed dozens of Europeans and Americans standing in the hallways. The foreigners looked dazed and tired. They had bags, suitcases, and boxes filled with clothes and papers.

Some of them called out to the hotel manager. But he walked past quickly.

"Why do you need my help?" Beth

asked him. She had to jog to keep up with him. "Can't someone on staff start the generator?"

Mr. Inumaru began to walk even faster. "My men are hard workers, but they don't understand electricity yet," he said. "They think the generator will restart the fires. The electric company is the building behind the Imperial Hotel. It exploded last night."

Beth shivered as she hurried along. "I saw the tornado fire," she said. "It was scary. I don't blame them for wanting to avoid another explosion."

Mr. Inumaru paused outside the kitchen door. "To be honest," he said, "I need someone who can read English well and squeeze under the stoves."

Beth grinned. "I'm only four feet tall," she said. "And I can read."

Mr. Inumaru pushed open the kitchen door.

Beth saw hotel staff workers standing at long tables. They were making little triangles of rice. Each rice treat was rolled in spices and then in seaweed.

Large metal trays were filled with rice balls. The trays covered nearly every empty counter. Several black electric ranges lined the walls. None of them were being used.

"This way," Mr. Inumaru said. He led Beth to the back of the kitchen. They stopped at a small wood door.

Mr. Inumaru turned the doorknob and opened the closet door.

Only a straw broom and a dirty apron hung from hooks on the wall. Otherwise it was empty.

"The generator is gone!" Mr. Inumaru cried.

Patrick stepped outside into the garden area of the hotel. So much had changed from the night before.

Tables and chairs lined the garden. They had been set up as a small wall to keep the refugees away. Guards dressed in uniform rode horses and carried rifles. Each rifle had a bayonet at the end of it.

The Japanese refugees were setting up camp. They clustered under the few trees that hadn't burned yet.

Green and tan tents stood in rows. They were lined up as far as Patrick could see. The people had their own little

stoves. They were cooking what food
they had.

Mr. Kagawa and several members of
the hotel staff stood behind a large table.
They were handing out rice balls. A line
of refugees stood waiting for the food.

Patrick took Chibi-chan over to one table.
They greeted Mr. Kagawa.

"Good morning," Mr. Kagawa said. "One
or two of the churches in the city didn't burn.
A missionary will be coming to take some of
the lost children."

Patrick hugged the little girl. His eyes
stung. He quickly rubbed them with one
hand. He would *not* cry. But giving Chibi-
chan away would be difficult.

"Why don't you take Chibi-chan into the
garden. See if you can find her family," Mr.
Kagawa said. "Then we will begin searching
for *your* parents."

"All right," Patrick said. He tried to sound calm even though he felt nervous. What if someone tried to take her again? He didn't speak Japanese. How would he know who her parents were?

Beth and Mr. Inumaru went through a side door. They walked out onto a patio. She grinned when she saw the generator. Mr. Inumaru groaned.

Two Japanese soldiers had the machine. It was open and lying on its side. The coils and wires were exposed.

The soldiers also had a large radio in a wood box. It had clear tubes with wires in it. One of the soldiers was trying to make something.

Beth thought he was trying to form a

homemade antenna. He was connecting scraps of metal and wires.

"The soldiers are trying to receive messages from ships more than eighteen miles away," Mr. Inumaru said. "Today information is more important than warm food. I wish them good fortune."

Beth said, "Maybe you can cook outside like you're camping."

The hotel manager nodded. "Go find your friend," he said. "Come back to help roll rice balls."

"I'll be back soon," Beth promised.

Beth found Mr. Kagawa. He told her that Patrick was looking for Chibi-chan's parents. Beth hurried to the refugee camp and found Patrick easily.

Her cousin was standing near three sumo wrestlers. The large men had their hair pulled back in ponytails.

One of the men held Chibi-chan. Then he tossed her in the air. She came down, and he caught her again.

Chibi-chan was laughing.

But Beth was nervous. What if the man dropped her?

Beth motioned for the man to hand over Chibi-chan. He gave her up slowly. Beth took the toddler and held her tight.

"Quick," Beth said to Patrick. "Let's say good-bye and leave."

Patrick leaned down and picked up Chibi-chan's blanket and doll.

"Where to?" Patrick asked.

"Those wrestlers didn't know her."

Suddenly a familiar noise sounded. It was like a trumpet blast.

"Zou!" Beth cried.

She turned and rushed toward the animal.

A group of children surrounded him. The animal's long trunk reached over to "kiss" one of them. They giggled and cheered.

One little boy stood back from the others.

Beth walked over to him to see what was wrong. Suddenly Chibi-chan began to talk in Japanese. Beth didn't understand her.

But the boy did. He rushed toward Beth.

"Miho," he said. He reached toward the child in Beth's arms.

Chibi-chan waved her doll.

The boy pulled something out of his pocket. Beth gasped.

It was a tiny wood toy. The second nesting doll.

Reunions

Patrick ran and got Mr. Kagawa. They came back to the crowd of refugees around the elephant.

Patrick saw Beth holding on to Chibi-chan. She was nodding to a Japanese woman and a man.

The woman's head was covered in a white scarf. The man had a hurt leg. A handmade wood crutch was under his left arm. His left leg was bandaged in an old blanket.

Mr. Kagawa spoke to the parents in Japanese. Patrick thought he heard the word *Jesus* a few times.

The man spoke the most. He made his hands look like a bridge. Then he pulled his hands apart.

Patrick whispered to Beth, "He's talking about the bridge falling."

"That's where you found Chibi-chan," Beth said. "She fell into your arms. Her parents must have been on the other side of the bridge."

Patrick said, "She didn't *fall*. She bounced toward me."

Mr. Kagawa motioned to Beth to hand over Chibi-chan. "I'm sure these are her parents," he said.

Patrick said, "I'm sure too. Miho and her brother have the doll set. How did the family get separated?"

Mr. Kagawa said, "They were on the bridge. Mr. Itō hurt his leg when he fell into a hole. Then the bridge moved and pinned it. Mrs. Itō put Miho down to help him. That's the last they saw of her until now."

"Wow," Beth said. "Thank God he's still alive."

"They are grateful," Mr. Kagawa said. "They agreed to come listen to more about Jesus. I told them He will care for Miho now and for all eternity."

An hour later the cousins were in the kitchen. Each wore an apron. Each was rolling rice balls.

"Four hundred and thirty-three," Patrick said. He placed a ball on a trav.

"Four hundred and thirty-four," Beth said. "Only nine

thousand five hundred sixty-six more to go."
She placed a rice ball on the tray.

Mr. Inumaru came through the side door of
the kitchen. His kind face was split into a wide
smile.

"You won't believe this," he said. "The US
Navy sent you a gift. It was made in America.
And so they thought it belonged at the US
embassy. But Mr. Kagawa said it belongs
to you. So they put it in the garden. Come
outside."

Beth and Patrick took off their aprons.

Patrick beat Beth to the patio.

Beth joined him. She took his hand and
squeezed it.

"It's the Imagination Station!" she cried.

Mr. Inumaru took a cloth out of his pocket.
He began to wipe down the old car.

The Imagination Station was covered in
sand and seaweed. The driver's-side door was

dented. The glass in the back was cracked in a spider-web design.

Beth's heart sank when she remembered it was broken.

"It doesn't have any battery power left," Patrick said. "It's useless."

"Have you tried cranking it up?" Mr. Inumaru asked.

Beth shook her head.

Mr. Inumaru went to the front of the car. He bent over and grabbed the crank. He churned it several times.

Suddenly a light came on inside the machine. Then a great burst of light exploded from the headlights.

Beth put her arm across her eyes to shield them from the brightness.

Mr. Inumaru shouted, "What! It can't be!"

Beth looked at the car.

Inside was a man. He was waving the

yellow electric gadget. He had thick, dark hair and a thick moustache. He wore a nice suit with a white shirt. He sat in the car with a smug expression on his face.

"It's Mr. Tesla!" Mr. Inumaru said.

**To find out about the next book
in the series, *Adventure in the Big Apple*,
visit TheImaginationStation.com.**

Secret Word Puzzle

The Great Kanto Earthquake of 1923 happened when three tectonic plates shifted at the same time. One of those plates was under the ocean. That caused a gigantic tsunami. A second plate pushed upward twenty-six feet. That caused the land to roll like waves.

A Japanese folktale explains earthquakes in a different way. The story tells about a giant creature trapped in the mud under the island. The earth moves if the creature gets loose and thrashes about. The name of that make-believe beast is the answer to the puzzle and the secret word.

Use the clues to fill in the puzzle on the next page. The letters in the shaded boxes will spell out the secret word. Write those letters in the boxes below the puzzle grid.

1. Food that Patrick and Beth helped roll into balls. Hint: page 74.

2. The American building that burned. Hint: page 62.

3. City where Patrick and Beth are in this adventure. Hint: pages 5, 60.

4. Something a wave or fast-moving water makes. Hint: pages 12, 21.

5. Last name of the crown prince. Hint: page 72.

6. Name of the Japanese religion mentioned at the temple. Hint: page 44.

7. Type of natural disaster that shook the Kanto region. Hint: pages 5, 135.

Secret Word Puzzle

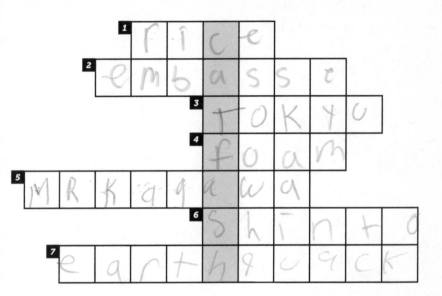

1. r i c e
2. e m b a s s e
3. T O K Y O
4. f o a m
5. M R K a g a w a
6. s h i n t o
7. e a r t h q u a c k

Answer:

1	2	3	4	5	6	7
C	a	T	F	i	S	h

Go to **TheImaginationStation.com.**
Find the cover of this book.
Click on "Secret Word."
**Type in the answer,
and you'll receive a prize.**

THE KEY TO ADVENTURE LIES WITHIN YOUR IMAGINATION.

OVER 750,000 SOLD IN SERIES

············ COLLECT ALL OF THEM TODAY! ············

AVAILABLE AT A CHRISTIAN RETAILER NEAR YOU

WWW.TYNDALE.COM

CP0674

JOIN AN EXCITING ADVENTURE FROM THE AWARD-WINNING
TEAM WHO BROUGHT YOU ADVENTURES IN ODYSSEY®!

Adventures in
ODYSSEY
CLUB™

All the fun and excitement of Adventures in
Odyssey now comes together with real-world
discipleship in an amazing club.

As a club member, you'll join Whit, Connie and your friends at
Whit's End as they learn what it means to follow Jesus. You'll
see how faith gets turned into action—from downtown Odyssey
to remote places around the world.

Check this out: you'll have access to exclusive stories, a special
website, discounts on lots of fun stuff and online streaming of
the entire library of more than 800 Adventures in Odyssey
episodes. It's inspiration and discipleship on-the-go!

Join the adventure at
aioclub.org